# MICHAEL GARLAND

# Miss Smith's Incredible Storybook

DUTTON CHILDREN'S BOOKS • NEW YORK

CIP Data is available.

Published in the United States by Dutton Children's Books,
a division of Penguin Putnam Books for Young Readers
345 Hudson Street, New York, New York 10014
www.penguin.com

Designed by Tim Hall  •  Manufactured in China
ISBN 0-525-47133-2
First Edition
3  5  7  9  10  8  6  4  2

To the teachers of St. Clare's School

It was the first day of school. Zack was waiting for his teacher to arrive.

Boring, boring . . . he thought. Why would this year be any different from the last one?

Then the door swung open.

"Good morning, class. My name is Miss Smith, and I am your new teacher."

$M$iss Smith seemed very . . . *different* from Zack's other teachers. But the day went along like every school day Zack could remember— until Miss Smith said, "It's story time."

When she sat at her desk and started to read from the book she had brought with her, Zack couldn't believe his eyes. The storybook characters came to life, and the classroom was swept up in a swashbuckling pirate tale.

Zack and the rest of his class were right in the middle of the story. He could feel the breeze in his hair and hear the waves pounding on the side of the ship.

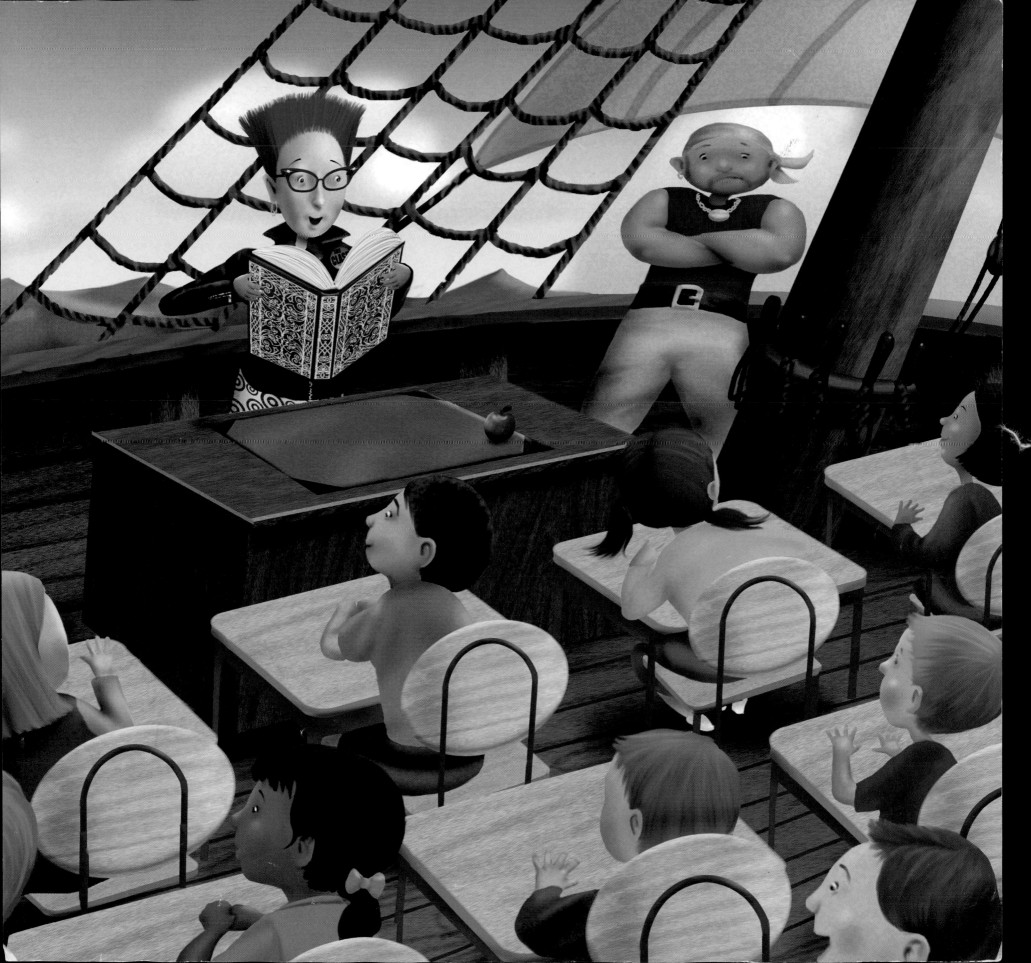

From then on, Zack couldn't wait to go to school. Every day there was a new story to look forward to. When Miss Smith finished reading, all the characters and adventure whooshed back into her book.

On Friday, Principal Rittenrotten stood in front of the class instead of Miss Smith.

"Miss Smith is stuck in traffic, so she has asked me to read to you until she arrives," he announced.

Zack wondered what would happen next.

Principal Rittenrotten started to read. Zack grinned when a princess leaped out of the book, followed closely by a fire-breathing dragon and a brave knight on his horse.

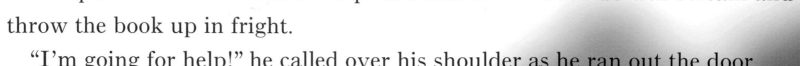

Principal Rittenrotten was so surprised that all he could do was scream and throw the book up in fright.

"I'm going for help!" he called over his shoulder as he ran out the door.

Before Zack could think of anything to do, Sue Ann pounced on the storybook.
But she didn't finish the dragon story—she started reading another one instead.
The princess, the dragon, and the knight did not return to the book,
but the Three Bears and Goldilocks climbed out!

**F**reddie, the class clown, jumped out of his seat and tried to yank the book away.
When Sue Ann let go, he tumbled backward, and the book flew across the room.
The whole class laughed.

**B**illy caught the book and started reading from a new story. Zack shook his head in amazement when the Mad Hatter, the Cheshire Cat, and Alice popped out to join the others.

As the book passed from kid to kid, one character after another flew out of the pages. The classroom was getting very crowded.

This is trouble, Zack said to himself. The chaos was beginning to spill out into the halls.

"Why don't you *finish* the stories?" Zack pleaded.

But no one was listening.

Miss Smith brought her car to a screeching stop in front of the school.
Uh-oh . . . there seems to be a little problem, she said to herself
as she raced inside.

Meanwhile, Zack was shouting, "We have to finish the stories so the characters will go back into the book!"

But the storybook characters didn't *want* to go back! A tug-of-war began.

Miss Smith appeared in the doorway. With one look, she let everyone know she meant business. Even the dragon was suddenly silent.

Zack handed the book back to Miss Smith. She ruffled through the pages, adjusted her glasses, and started to read. The class sat spellbound as she finished each story in turn. With a swirl and a whoosh, one character after another disappeared into the book, until the classroom was quiet and tidy again.

Principal Rittenrotten and a team of firefighters skidded to a halt at the door, just as Miss Smith closed her book.

"May I help you, Principal Rittenrotten?" asked Miss Smith.

But the principal couldn't seem to answer. He just stared at the quiet class with his mouth wide open.

Miss Smith flashed a secret smile at her class. Zack smiled right back. Who would ever have guessed that reading could be so much fun?

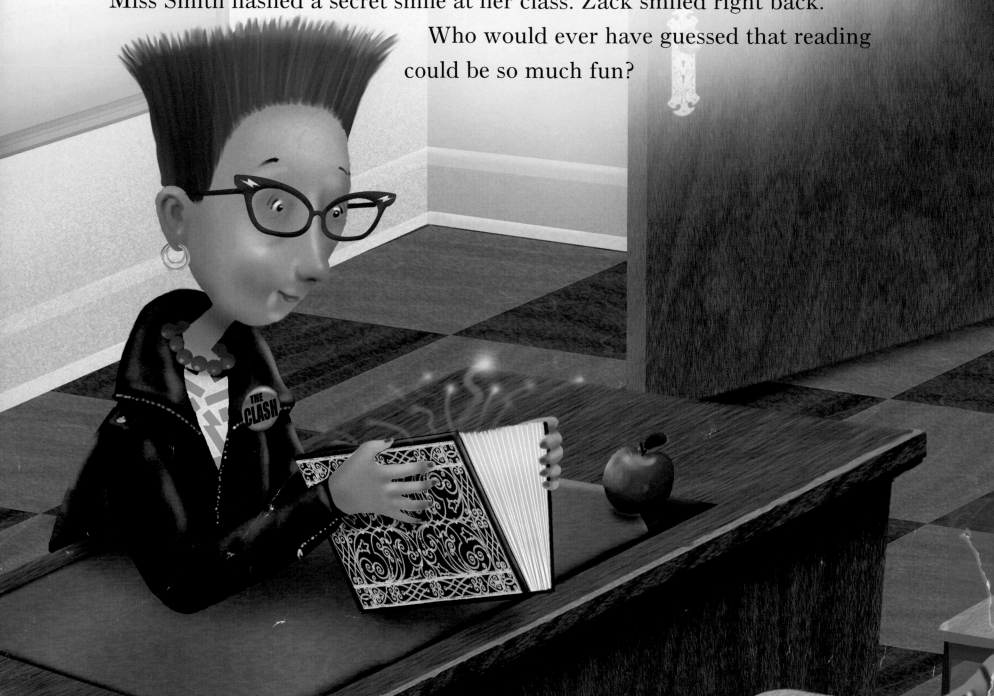